ANIMALS
ON
THE EDGE
TIGER

ANIMALS ON THE EDGE
TIGER

by Anna Claybourne

BLOOMSBURY

LONDON   BERLIN   NEW YORK   SYDNEY

Published 2012 by
Bloomsbury Publishing Plc
50 Bedford Square, London, WC1B 3DP

www.bloomsbury.com

ISBN HB 978-1-4081-4824-2
ISBN PB 978-1-4081-4957-7

Picture acknowledgements:
Cover: Shutterstock
Insides: All Shutterstock except for the following; p7 third inset from bottom ©Shanghai
Gallery via Wikimedia Commons, p 8 bottom ©Meister des Madhu-Malati-Manuskripts
via Wikimedia Commons, p11 top inset ©Dan Bennett via Wikimedia Commons, p11
bottom inset ©Victoria and Albert Museum via Wikimedia Commons, p13 top inset ©ZSL/
James Godwin, p14 all images ©ZSL, p15 bottom inset ©ZSL, p16 bottom ©Nature Picture
Library/Anup Shah, p17 top ©ZSL, pp18-19 all images ©ZSL, p21 bottom ©ZSL, p22
©ZSL, p24 ©Ernst Stavro Blofeld via Wikimedia Commons, p25 top © Laymens68 (Own
work) via Wikimedia Commons, p27 top ©ZSL/Adam Barlow/WTB, p28 ©D Chapagain/
Wildlife Conservation Nepal, p29 top ©IFAW via www.nfwf.org, p29 bottom ©Banks EIA/
WPSI, p30 ©ZSL, p31 top ©ZSL/Monirul Khan, p33 all images ©ZSL, p34 all images
©ZSL, p35 top ©ZSL, p37 all images ©ZSL, p38 logo ©RSPO, p40 ©Andries Hoogerwerf,
via Wikimedia Commons, p41 top ©ZSL

Manufactured and supplied under licence from the Zoological Society of London.

Produced for Bloomsbury Publishing Plc by Geoff Ward.

A CIP catalogue for this book is available from the British Library.

Printed in China by C&C Offset Printing Co.

CONTENTS

MEET THE TIGER

The tiger is a big cat. In fact, it's the biggest of *all* wild cats. A tiger can be five times as long as a domestic (pet) cat, and up to 50 times heavier. A domestic cat can jump from the ground onto a two-metre-high fence, but a tiger can jump five metres straight up and could easily leap onto the roof of a house! With its black and orange stripes, golden-green eyes and mighty roar, it's also one of the most striking, beautiful animals on Earth.

Jaws, paws and claws

Like all cats, tigers are meat-eaters, and they are built for hunting. They have long, sharp teeth, and big feet with huge, curved claws. Their legs are strong and springy, for leaping onto prey, and their long tails help them balance.

When a tiger roars, you can see the huge, sharp teeth it uses for tearing at meat.

DO TIGERS BEHAVE LIKE PET CATS?

Tigers lick their paws and curl up to sleep, just like smaller cats. In other ways, however, they're very different. For example, tigers make a "chuffing" noise (like a puff of air) instead of purring. And most domestic cats hate water, but tigers love it.

ASIA

On this map, the areas in yellow show where tigers live in the wild.

The six tigers

There is only one main **species**, or type of tiger, but it is divided into six **subspecies**, which all live in different parts of Asia (except for the South China tiger which is sadly now **extinct** in the wild).

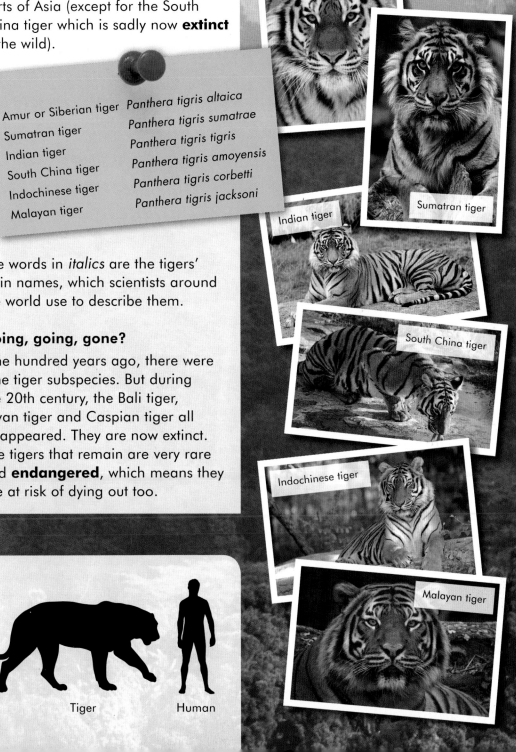

Amur or Siberian tiger

Amur or Siberian tiger — *Panthera tigris altaica*
Sumatran tiger — *Panthera tigris sumatrae*
Indian tiger — *Panthera tigris tigris*
South China tiger — *Panthera tigris amoyensis*
Indochinese tiger — *Panthera tigris corbetti*
Malayan tiger — *Panthera tigris jacksoni*

The words in *italics* are the tigers' Latin names, which scientists around the world use to describe them.

Going, going, gone?

One hundred years ago, there were nine tiger subspecies. But during the 20th century, the Bali tiger, Javan tiger and Caspian tiger all disappeared. They are now extinct. The tigers that remain are very rare and **endangered**, which means they are at risk of dying out too.

Sumatran tiger

Indian tiger

South China tiger

Indochinese tiger

Malayan tiger

Tiger   Human

TIGERS ON THE EDGE

A long time ago, tigers roamed all over the vast continent of Asia, and its many islands. Today, places where tigers still live make up less than five per cent of that area. One hundred years ago, it's thought there were at least 100,000 tigers living in the wild. Now there are only around 4,000 to 5,000.

What happened?

There are two main reasons so many tigers have disappeared: hunting and **habitat loss**. **Habitat** means the wild, natural surroundings where an animal likes to live. For tigers, that's mainly forests. People have cut down forests for wood, and to make space for homes, farms and roads. Now, there's not much left for tigers.

Cutting down trees for their wood leaves the land bare, with fewer forest areas for wildlife to live in.

People also hunt tigers, for their skins, and for other body parts, which they use to make medicines. Sometimes, people also kill tigers to stop them from killing farm animals, or even humans.

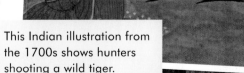

This Indian illustration from the 1700s shows hunters shooting a wild tiger.

What can we do?

Lots of wildlife charities and **conservation** groups around the world are trying to save tigers from dying out, such as 21st Century Tiger and ZSL (the Zoological Society of London). As well as running projects in the wild to try and protect tigers, ZSL keeps Sumatran and Amur tigers at its two zoos, ZSL London Zoo and ZSL Whipsnade Zoo.

ON THE RED LIST

The **IUCN**, or International Union for Conservation of Nature, keeps a list of living things and how endangered they are, called the "IUCN red list". All six types of tigers are on it.

Amur tiger — Endangered (at risk of dying out)

Sumatran tiger — Critically endangered

Indian tiger — Endangered

South China tiger — Critically endangered (and extinct in the wild)

Indochinese tiger — Endangered

Malayan tiger — Endangered

An armed guard protects wildlife by watching out for hunters.

BIG, FIERCE AND RARE

Tigers are big, fierce **predators** – they hunt other animals. So it seems strange that they should be in so much danger. In fact, big hunting animals like tigers are the ones that suffer most from hunting and habitat loss. They need lots of space, so that they can wander around and find their prey. And it takes a lot of **prey** animals to feed one tiger.

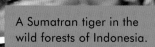

A Sumatran tiger in the wild forests of Indonesia.

TIGER TALES

Although people have often hunted tigers, these huge cats have also been respected and admired. In myths and legends, they are seen as the bravest and strongest of animals, and in many Asian folktales, the tiger, not the lion, is the king of the jungle.

The tiger-riding goddess

In the Hindu religion, Durga is a powerful, but kind goddess. She stands for energy and goodness, and she can defeat any evil. She has 18 arms, and rides on a tiger's back. According to Hindu books, the other gods created Durga to fight a terrible demon, Mahishasura, that no one else could conquer. Riding her tiger, she killed him with her sword, after freezing him to the spot with a glowing light.

An Indian illustration of Durga, with her many arms and tiger transport.

Old Indian art often shows people riding tigers, though it wouldn't be very sensible!

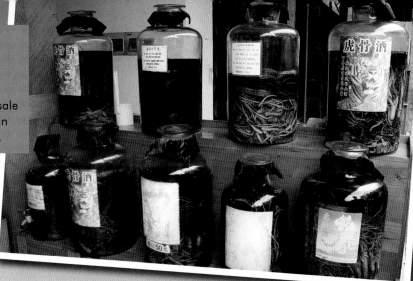

Traditional medicines made from endangered animals for sale in a market in Burma, Asia.

Power and energy

You'll see the tiger used in logos and symbols for all kinds of products, especially those that give energy, like fuel oil and breakfast cereal. There are countless tigers in children's books and cartoons. They are exciting, colourful and fierce, but often funny too. Tigers may be rare, and only found in Asia, but they are popular with people all over the world, and people love going to see them in zoos.

Magic powers

In some parts of Asia, especially China, the tiger is thought to be so powerful that its body parts can cure illnesses. Tiger bones, teeth, eyeballs, claws, whiskers and other body parts are used to make **traditional** medicines, even though scientists think that tiger parts have no medicinal or magical properties. This is one big reason why people still try to hunt tigers, even though it is now banned.

THE TIGER-CRAZY SULTAN

Tipu **Sultan** was a famous ruler of Mysore, a kingdom in India, in the 1700s. He admired tigers so much that he made the tiger his personal symbol. He decorated his flags, weapons and armour with tiger pictures and tiger stripes. He even had a musical robot tiger made for him! Tipu Sultan also is known for his famous saying: "In this world I would rather live two days like a tiger, than two hundred years like a sheep".

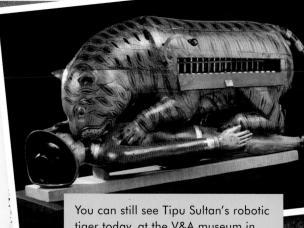

You can still see Tipu Sultan's robotic tiger today, at the V&A museum in London. The wooden tiger moves, makes noises and attacks a soldier!

THE TIGER AT HOME

Asia is very big, and wild tigers are very rare, so it's hard to spot them. But they are still there, living in the small, broken-up areas of natural habitat that are still left.

At home in the forests

In the wild, tigers live in all kinds of forests. Some live in thick, steamy rainforests, some in dry, cool forests, some in snowy mountain forests, and some in dense **bamboo** forests. Some tigers also live in more open, grassland areas. In India and Bangladesh, a lot of Indian tigers live in **mangrove** forests. These are swampy forests of mangrove trees, which grow along the edges of rivers or the sea, with their roots in the water.

Tiger territory

Tigers are **solitary** – they usually live alone. But they do meet up to mate, and sometimes to play together or share food. Each adult tiger has its own **territory**. It patrols around its territory and marks it with urine, droppings, scratch marks on trees, and special scent markings. It guards its territory against most other tigers, so that it can keep the **prey** animals in that area for itself.

TIGER SIGNS

You can sometimes tell how a tiger feels from its body language:
- Ears twisted around – on edge and ready for danger
- Tail low down and twitching – annoyed
- Tail swishing – excited or **aggressive**
- Tail up and waving – happy and friendly

Tigers have black and white "eye-spots" on the backs of their ears.

A tiger's day

Like a pet cat, a tiger spends most of a typical day snoozing, lounging around and relaxing – as much as 18 hours out of every 24. But tigers aren't lazy. They do this to save energy, so that they have enough left to go hunting.

Tigers sometimes hunt during the day, but mainly at dusk or at night. They can prowl around very slowly and quietly, following the sound of their prey, until they get close enough to pounce.

Tigers have good eyesight and can see well in the dark.

A Siberian tiger takes a refreshing swim in a river.

SPLASHING TIGER

A lot of tigers live in very hot countries. They like to cool down by lying in a pond or river, or even going for a splash in the sea!

TIGERS IN THE ZOO

Now that tigers have become so rare, there are actually more tigers in captivity, such as zoos, than there are in the wild. Keeping tigers in zoos is incredibly important. It could be the only way the tiger can keep going as a species.

A tiger enclosure

An **enclosure** is the fenced area that a zoo animal lives in. Tigers have a strong urge to wander around, so their enclosures have to be quite big. Tigers also like to be surrounded by lots of interesting plants and trees. They need a pool to swim and wallow in, and some sheltered areas where they can hide. Tigers also like to climb and be high up, so they can get a good look around. So their enclosure might have special climbing logs or rocks too.

An Amur tiger relaxes on a high platform at ZSL Whipsnade Zoo.

Part of ZSL London Zoo's Sumatran tiger enclosure, with covered dens, plants and trees.

Something to do

Tigers like to have lots to do. So to keep them busy, the keepers give them different toys every day, such as balls hanging on ropes, unbreakable floating balls in the pool, and sacks stuffed with hay for them to pounce on and tear to bits.

Tigers also love sniffing out different smells, so the keepers sprinkle scents onto the sacks and around the enclosure. They use ginger, curry powder, herbs, or perfumes.

Helping tigers

Zoos all over the world keep tigers, so that scientists can learn more about them and help their populations to grow through breeding programmes. Zoos are also important because they help educate people about tigers and raise money for conservation projects to help protect wild tigers.

A Sumatran tiger in **captivity** enjoys a game with a floating ball at Los Angeles Zoo, USA.

Zoos try to recreate elements of the tiger's wild habitat, where it can roam and explore.

HALLOWEEN TIGER FUN

At many zoos, zookeepers like to give the tigers seasonal toys. In the autumn at Halloween, they give them pumpkins to play with, which the tigers like to prod, lick and smell.

WHAT TIGERS EAT

Tigers are brilliant hunting, killing and eating machines. They are so strong, they can kill prey much bigger than themselves, such as a moose or buffalo. They are apex predators, **which means they eat a lot of other animals, but nothing really eats them.**

Tiger menu

A tiger's favourite foods are usually wild pigs and deer. But, depending on where they live, tigers also eat buffalos and gaurs (a type of cow), antelopes, farm sheep and goats, large snakes, young rhinos and even young elephants. They also snap up smaller snacks, like birds, monkeys, fish or crabs.

When a tiger makes a kill, it will eat as much of the animal as it can, as it may not have another meal for a few days.

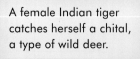

A female Indian tiger catches herself a chital, a type of wild deer.

Going hunting

To hunt its prey, a tiger mainly uses its ears to hear a pig snuffling around, or an antelope rustling through the bushes. When it gets close enough to see its target, the tiger crouches down. Silently, it creeps closer and closer... then POUNCES! A large tiger can leap as far as ten metres – almost the length of a bus – along the ground. However, for every ten hunts, a tiger only catches prey once. Usually, the animal is startled and runs away in time.

Feeding time at the zoo

In the zoo, tigers don't get to catch and eat living animals. Instead they are fed whole pieces of animal, including the hair and bones. The keepers sometimes scatter the meat around for the tigers, then let them in to eat it. Or they feed them through the enclosure bars, using special feeding tongs. Keepers never go into the same area as the tigers as it's too dangerous.

Feeding tongs let zookeepers put food right into a tiger's mouth, in safety!

DO TIGERS EAT PEOPLE?

Yes, they do. Most tigers prefer other meat, and will only attack humans if they feel threatened. But occasionally individual tigers start to see humans as easy targets – especially the Indian tigers in the Sundarbans area of India and Bangladesh (see page 32).

NIGHT VISION

Like many hunting animals, tigers have good night vision. At the back of their eyes is a silvery layer, like a mirror, called the **tapetum lucidum**. It reflects light back out of the tiger's eyes, so that twice as much light passes through the eye's light-detecting **cells**. This helps tigers to see when there's only a small amount of light.

Light reflected from the tapetum lucidum is what makes tigers' (and other cats') eyes seem to glow with light at night.

A DAY IN THE LIFE: TIGER KEEPER

Paul Kybett is a Senior Keeper at ZSL London Zoo. He looks after the Sumatran tigers there, as well as some of the other animals. He explains what happens on a typical day as a zookeeper.

Paul in his green ZSL London Zoo uniform.

A day with the tigers

8.00am The first job of the day is to get the meat joints out of the fridge. We add a **vitamin** supplement and a bit of cod liver oil to the meat, to help keep the tigers healthy. Then we head over to the tiger exhibit and call the tigers into their indoor area. We feed them separately: Lumpur usually gets his food first, followed by Reika, to avoid any arguments.

9.00am While the tigers are eating their breakfast, we go out into their **paddock**, or outdoor area. We clean it, lay down new straw in the shelters, and do a bit of gardening, such as weeding and pruning the trees. This is also the time to give the windows a wash, and to put out new **enrichment** such as balls, or sacks sprinkled with ground ginger.

Changing the tigers' straw beds is hard work, but it has to be done every day.

Paul expertly scoops up a fresh tiger poo using a shovel.

10.00am It's time to let the tigers out, while we move on to scrubbing their indoor enclosure. We clear up the remains of their breakfast, change their straw bed, and refill their water.

2.00pm Time for lunch! We bring the tigers inside, separate them, and feed them meat through the mesh using tongs. While they're safely inside, we also scatter meat around in their paddock. We let them out at 2.30pm, just in time for our tiger talk for the zoo visitors.

5.30pm We say goodnight to our tigers before going home. During the night, our tigers are free to roam around both their indoor and outdoor enclosures.

TIGER TOILET

Like all meat-eaters, tigers have horribly smelly poo! We use a shovel to clear it out. Luckily our tigers prefer to poo in the same spots every time, which makes the job a little easier.

BEST BITS AND WORST BITS!

I love calling the tigers in for their morning breakfast, which they're always excited about. I also really like working with tigers as they are quiet and relatively calm animals. I'm not too keen on working with hectic, noisy animals such as chimps. But there's one job I don't like – changing the tiger's beds. All that straw and hay gets right up my nose!

Lumpur, the male tiger at ZSL London Zoo, is a beautiful Sumatran tiger.

TIGER CUBS

Although a male tiger will keep other males away from his territory, he will share with females. Male and female territories overlap, so that they can meet up to mate and breed, or have cubs.

Cute cubs!

When tigers are looking for a mate, they call to each other with howling and whining noises. They only meet up for a short time. After mating, they go off alone again. The mother gives birth to her cubs nearly three months later, in a **den** such as a cave, a gap between rocks, or a space between bushes.

There are usually two or three tiger cubs in a **litter**. They are born blind, with their eyes closed. For the first few weeks, they stay in the den and feed only on milk. Tigers are **mammals**, which means the mother makes milk in her body for her babies to drink.

When a male and female tiger meet up to mate, they often play together and nuzzle each other.

This fluffy little tiger cub is just a few weeks old, and its head looks very big for its body!

Tiger cubs love jumping around and play-fighting with each other, and with their mum.

Growing and learning

As they get older, the cubs start to follow their mum and watch her hunting. They learn to hunt by play-fighting and pouncing on each other, or on their mum's tail! Sometimes they practise hunting on flowers or insects.

In the zoo

To breed tigers in the zoo, keepers put a male and a female together in the same enclosure. As long as they have spaces where they can spend time alone, they are usually happy together. Zoos have bred a lot of tigers successfully. As tiger cubs are so cute and cuddly, people love coming to see them.

FACT FILE: GROWING UP

Gestation (how long the cubs take to grow before birth): 13-16 weeks

Weight at birth: 1-2 kilos

2 weeks: Cubs open their eyes

6-7 weeks: They start eating meat caught by their mum.

8 weeks: They start to leave the den.

2 years: Cubs are ready to leave their mum and go off alone.

4 years: The cubs are adults, and can find a mate of their own.

As they get older, the cubs spend more time alone.

DID YOU KNOW?

Other animals don't eat adult tigers, but some animals, such as snakes, wolves and bears, sometimes hunt tiger cubs.

TWO TIGERS' STORIES: LUMPUR AND REIKA

Lumpur and Reika are Sumatran tigers living in ZSL London Zoo. They are a perfect match for each other, and are best friends.

Getting together

Lumpur was born in a French Zoo in 1997. He moved to ZSL London Zoo in 1999, aged two. There, he met Reika, a female tiger already living in London. She was born in Berlin Zoo in 1995, and came to ZSL London Zoo in 1997. The two tigers have always got on brilliantly together. They always greet each other by making a chuffing noise.

A change of plan

The keepers had put Lumpur and Reika together so that they could breed – but after a few years, they still hadn't had babies. So ZSL came up with a new idea. In 2006, they swapped Reika with another female, called Sarah, from Dudley Zoo near Birmingham UK. They hoped that Lumpur and Sarah would breed instead.

Lumpur and Reika are both calm, serious tigers, and don't like making a fuss or running around.

Sumatra, where Sumatran tigers live in the wild, is one of Indonesia's largest islands.

SUMATRA

Indian Ocean

Who are you?

Unfortunately, Lumpur and Sarah were very different tigers. At Dudley Zoo, Sarah and her male mate were always play-fighting and stalking each other. But Lumpur and Reika are much more serious tigers! When Sarah tried to play-fight with Lumpur, he wasn't impressed, and they began to fall out. In Dudley, the same thing happened. Reika did not like her new mate either.

Together again

After a year and a half of being separated, the zoos decided to try another approach, and moved Reika back to ZSL London Zoo. Lumpur and Reika were delighted to see each other again — and they've been living happily together ever since.

SUMATRAN TIGERS

Sumatran tigers come from Sumatra, an island that's part of the country of Indonesia. They are quite different from other tiger subspecies. They tend to be darker in colour, smaller and sleeker than other tigers. There are not many Sumatran tigers left in the wild — only around 300.

Sumatran tigers have shaggy fur around their faces, a bit like a lion's mane.

WHAT'S LUMPUR LIKE?

Lumpur is a friendly tiger, but not *too* friendly. He's quite comfortable around his keepers, and doesn't bat an eyelid when they approach him, showing he's relaxed and content. But he is quite serious, and sometimes a bit grumpy. He's a quiet tiger, and loves to sleep.

THREATS TO TIGERS

Here you can find out a bit more about why tigers are so endangered. They face many different problems, and these all add up to a very serious situation.

Poaching

Poaching means hunting that is not allowed. The tiger is a protected species, and hunting it is banned in most countries – but some people still do it. To the poachers, it's worth the risk of being caught, because they can make so much money from a dead tiger. They can sell many parts of its body for making medicines. And in some places, people still want to buy tiger fur, and tiger skins, to use as a **status symbol** in their homes.

Trophy hunting

Trophy hunting for "sport" is hunting big wild animals. Long ago, especially in India, it was seen as manly and brave to kill a tiger. People would hunt tigers, then take them home and have them stuffed, or made into tiger-skin rugs. Thousands of tigers died this way. Some trophy hunting still happens, even though it's not allowed.

Lord Curzon, a British ruler in India over 100 years ago, and his wife Mary stand proudly over a tiger he has killed.

Losing land

Tigers have suffered badly from habitat loss (losing their natural habitats). This is partly because many Asian countries, especially China and India, have a lot of people. All those people need places to live, farms to grow food, and wood for building and burning. So they cut down more and more forests.

Farms, roads, railways and cities have also divided tiger habitat up into smaller and smaller areas. This is called **habitat fragmentation**. It's bad news for tigers as it means they can't roam long distances or meet other tigers to mate.

No room for tigers

As the human **population** grows, people and tigers end up living closer to each other. People fear tigers, because they can be killers. They also eat farm animals, or wild animals that humans want to hunt. For these reasons, people sometimes shoot tigers just to get rid of them.

In the past, sometimes tigers' heads were stuffed and hung on the wall to show them off.

Traditional tiger-skin rugs often included the tiger's stuffed head.

CLEVER EARS

Tigers are clever animals, with very sensitive ears. In the past, when tigers were hunted mercilessly with rifles, some tigers learned to associate the sound of a gun being loaded with trouble, and run away.

HOW CAN WE HELP TIGERS?

Tigers face many problems, but there are lots of ways we can help them. Many conservation charities are all working together to try to save the tigers we still have from dying out.

Save the forest

Tigers can't survive in the wild without their natural habitat – the forests. Some schemes work with **governments** and the **logging** companies that cut down forests, to agree on which areas of forest to leave for tigers and other wildlife.

Saving forests, like this one in Thailand, from being cut down can help tigers to survive.

Parks and reserves

The government of a country can set aside a piece of land as a **national park** or **wildlife reserve**. In these areas, no one is allowed to hunt, build, farm, cut down trees or disturb wildlife. There are already lots of parks and reserves around the world, but we need more in Asian countries to help tigers survive.

TIGER CHALLENGE

Helping tigers can be hard work! They often live in remote jungle areas, and can be dangerous. Poachers often carry guns, and don't like anyone interfering in their business. Conservation projects need brave, devoted workers, and plenty of money, to succeed.

Stop the hunting

Hunting tigers is banned, but it still happens. To stop it, there must be strict laws and punishments, and ways to find and catch the poachers. One way to help is to make protected areas more secure, with lots of **park rangers** to patrol them and look out for poachers.

Help the humans

People kill tigers mainly because they need money, or want to protect their farm animals and families. So some conservation projects work on ways to keep tigers out of villages, such as using smoke and noisy rattles. There are also teams that can catch troublemaking tigers and move them somewhere safer.

Working in conservation can provide a good income for local people in the areas where tigers live.

Tourists can visit this tiger in a zoo in Thailand, where tigers also live in the wild.

Spread the message

Inspiring people is really important for saving endangered species. Public campaigns help people understand that tigers are close to dying out, and that they may be worth more alive than dead. Slowly, many people are realising that traditional tiger medicines are old-fashioned, bad for tigers, and have no special powers or medicinal benefits.

THE POACHING PROBLEM

It might be hard to imagine wanting to kill a beautiful, rare tiger. But for some people, it's how they make a living. Of course, there's a big problem with that! If the poaching carries on, there will soon be no tigers left.

How many tigers?

Experts think that poachers probably kill at least one tiger *every day*, somewhere in Asia. Remember, there are probably fewer than 4,000 tigers left in the wild – so that's almost one in every ten tigers being killed each year.

How much money?

Prices for tiger parts for traditional medicines are getting higher. This is partly because many Asian countries, where tiger parts are sold, have grown richer in the past 20 years, and so people have more money to spend. A trader can sometimes make the same amount of money from selling tiger parts as he would earn in ten years doing a normal job. When it's sold as a medicine, one kilo of tiger bone can cost the equivalent of between £200 and £2,000.

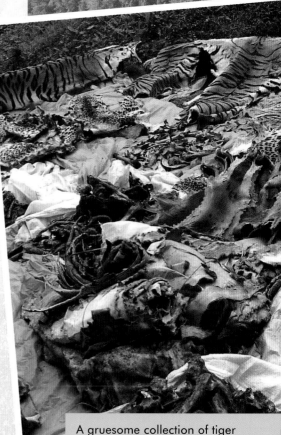

A gruesome collection of tiger skins, bones and other body parts confiscated from poachers in Nepal.

Traditional medicines, such as tiger bone wine, for sale in a shop in China.

How do poachers catch tigers?

- **Snares** The poachers make a wire loop to fit a tiger's foot or head, and attach it to a small, bent-over tree. When the tiger gets caught in the snare, it triggers the tree to spring up, pulling the snare tight.
- **Traps** The poachers build a cage and put a bait, such as a pig, inside. However, they prefer snares, as setting up a trap takes a long time.
- **Poison** Poachers fill a dead deer with poison, or put poison on a dead animal that a tiger hasn't finished eating.
- **Shooting** Some poachers shoot tigers, though this is less common.

THE TIGER MARKET

It's not just the poachers that are the problem - it's the people who buy the dead tiger parts, make them into medicines, and sell them on so they end up in shops and markets. All this is banned in most countries, but people still do it in secret – this is known as the "**black market**".

Tiger skins and other wild animal skins on sale in a market in Tibet.

HELPING AMUR TIGERS

The Amur or Siberian tiger is only found in the far east of Russia, where it borders the Pacific Ocean. In this area, the Zoological Society of London (ZSL) works at a protected area called the Lazovsky State Nature Reserve. Amur tigers are thriving there, but they are at serious risk from poachers.

Tiger tracking

To help tigers, it's important to monitor them, which means counting them, and keeping track of where they go. This helps us find out what tigers most need to survive, and where to look out for poachers.

Amur tigers have big territories and like to wander far and wide. Instead of tracking tigers, ZSL use **camera traps** to "watch" them. They set up automatic cameras along the tigers' trails. When a tiger comes close enough, it triggers the camera to take a picture.

This Amur tiger was captured by a hidden camera in the Lazovsky State Nature Reserve.

Watching the hunters

The tigers often wander between two areas of protected land, through an area where hunting deer and other animals is allowed. Here, they could be shot accidentally, or caught by poachers. So the workers put plenty of camera traps on this route. As well as monitoring the tigers, the idea of being caught on camera helps to put the poachers off.

More to eat

Amur tigers are normally very spread out in the wild, but in the Lazovsky reserve, they can live closer together. The reserve keeps the number of wild deer and pigs in the park as high as possible. This extra food means that more tigers can live there, have more cubs, and increase their numbers.

Up and down

In the early 1900s, thanks to hunting and habitat loss, Amur tigers almost died out. Less than 50 animals remained in the wild. Protecting them has helped them recover, and there are now about 350 of them.

A ZSL worker puts a camera in place in a tiger reserve.

Eastern Siberia has a lot of very remote, wild and empty land that is very good for tigers.

ECOTOURISM

Ecotourism means going to see wildlife as a tourist. It can help to bring in money for conservation. The Lazovsky Reserve makes extra money from film crews, scientists, and tourists who pay to visit the reserve, stay there and be shown around by wildlife guides. Ecotourism helps local people too, by giving them jobs.

ONE TIGER'S STORY: SUNDARBANS RESCUE

The Sundarbans is a huge area of swamps and mangrove forests. It lies along the coast of India and Bangladesh, where several rivers join together and flow into the Indian Ocean. Many wildlife charities have been working here to help solve problems between local people and Indian tigers.

Man-eaters

The Sundarbans area is known for its aggressive tigers, which regularly attack people. They're known as "man-eating" tigers, but it's often children who get caught. No one knows exactly why this happens so much in the Sundarbans. But it means that local villagers are very scared of tigers. If one comes close to a village, they often chase it with long sticks, surround it and sometimes beat it to death, before it can harm anyone.

The Indian tiger is seen as a very "typical"-looking tiger. It's large, vivid orange with black stripes, and has a large head and powerful jaws.

A tiger in town!

One example was a large female Indian tiger who entered a village in Bangladesh, on the borders of the Sundarbans. Soon after she was seen swimming in a local canal, a crowd gathered, ready to defend their village. But instead of being killed, this tiger was rescued and moved away, keeping both her and the villagers safe. But how?

Tiger team to the rescue

The solution to situations like this is a tiger response team, made up of local wildlife officers, vets and volunteers. They have been set up by the Bangladeshi government, with help from wildlife charities. Whenever a tiger appears, villagers can call the team to come and help.

A tiger is spotted on the prowl at night, close to a village.

Safely asleep, the tiger can be given a health check and moved out of harm's way.

What happened?

- When the team arrived, they began to reassure the villagers, and help the crowd to calm down.
- They quickly put the tiger to sleep with a safe **tranquilising drug**.
- They worked together to carry the tiger onto a boat, where she was held safely in a cabin.
- The boat carried the tiger away, deep into the jungle, to be released.
- As she slept, the team checked the tiger over for injuries.
- When she woke up, the tiger was given a snack of four chickens, then set free into the jungle.

CONSERVATION BREEDING

Conservation breeding **means helping animals to breed, or have babies, in captivity** – especially in zoos. As all types of tigers are the same species, they could all breed with each other. But to keep the subspecies as they are in the wild, zoos breed each one separately.

Staying alive

Conservation breeding is important for tigers, as there are so few of them left in the wild. Its keeps a healthy population alive in zoos, and makes sure there are always more tigers to replace them. Conservation breeding helps scientists too, as they can study closely how tigers breed, and what conditions they need. They can then use what they learn to help tigers in the wild.

Hari, a Sumatran tiger cub born at ZSL London Zoo in 1996.

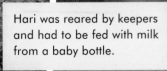

Hari was reared by keepers and had to be fed with milk from a baby bottle.

Matching pairs

To make sure tigers have healthy babies, they need to be moved around and matched up in pairs from different families. For strong, healthy cubs, the two tiger parents should be unrelated. A tiger should not mate with a member of its own family, as this can lead to cubs being born with illnesses.

Zoos keep careful records of all the tigers born in captivity, and who their parents are. They find pairs of tigers that make a good match, and move them around so that they can live together and mate. This list of tigers and breeding information is known as a **studbook**.

Hari snuggles in his straw bed, curling up just as smaller cats do.

Eventually, Hari moved to Australia, and became a father to a female cub, named Sali.

TIGER SOS!

Tiger SOS is the name of a campaign run by ZSL to raise money for its tiger conservation projects in the wild, as well as building a brilliant new Sumatran tiger enclosure at ZSL London Zoo.

A new home

The new exhibit will recreate an area of Sumatran rainforest for the zoo tigers, along with sheltered areas. Besides being a better enclosure for them, it will help visitors to experience what the tigers' wild habitat is like, and learn about how they live in the wild.

Staff at ZSL are working hard to raise money for the Tiger SOS campaign.

Give Tigers a Tomorrow

Wild Sumatran rainforest is thick, dense and damp.

MAKING THE MONEY

A new exhibit like this costs a lot of money – at least £3 million. The Tiger SOS campaign is working to raise money from public donations, businesses and sponsored events.

Zoos of the future

You already learn a lot about animals when you go to the zoo. But at ZSL London Zoo, and other zoos following the same development plans, you'll be able to go to talks about wild animals, meet zoo keepers at special events, and visit in a school group to do conservation activities. This approach helps zoos to teach people as much as possible about wildlife conservation, as well as simply giving them amazing wild animals to look at.

The new ZSL London Zoo tiger exhibit will be much more like Lumpur and Reika's Sumatran jungle home.

You could visit Lumpur the tiger at ZSL London Zoo, or adopt him.

What can you do?

- **Visit ZSL London Zoo** It's a fun day out, and every visit raises money for conservation projects and campaigns.
- **Join a fundraising event** Look on the Zoo's website for information about sponsored fun runs and other events.
- **Adopt a tiger** You can adopt a tiger and get regular updates about how it's doing.

HELPING SUMATRAN TIGERS

The rare, beautiful and unusual Sumatran tiger is one of the tiger subspecies conservationists are working hard to help. Several projects are being run in Sumatra, Indonesia to try to protect tiger habitat, and help local people live alongside wild tigers more easily.

Palm oil problems

In parts of Indonesia, people grow **oil palms** to make money. The oil from them is used in all kinds of products, from chocolate to make-up. But to grow the palm trees, farmers have to clear away wild forests – the natural habitat of tigers and many other animals. The palm plantations also split up remaining forest areas into sections, so tigers can't move from one area to another.

Palm plans

One ZSL project works with the palm farmers to try to grow plantations on land that won't disturb tigers as much, and agree to leave some areas of forest wild, with strips of forest, called **wildlife corridors**, to join them together. If they do this, they can put a "**sustainable** palm oil" label on their product. People who buy things made with the oil can see that it has been grown in a wildlife-friendly way.

If you see this logo on something you buy, you know it comes from a wildlife-friendly palm plantation.

CERTIFIED SUSTAINABLE PALM OIL ™

· RSPO ·

Poacher patrols

Organisations like ZSL also raise money for poacher patrols in Berbak National Park, on the east coast of Sumatra. This park contains swampy forests that are a perfect habitat for the Sumatran tiger. But it has problems with poachers around the area, illegal logging and people starting fires.

The poacher patrol teams are made up of small groups of soldiers, who follow the tigers' trails through the forest. They check on the tigers, look out for snares and dismantle them, and arrest any poachers they catch.

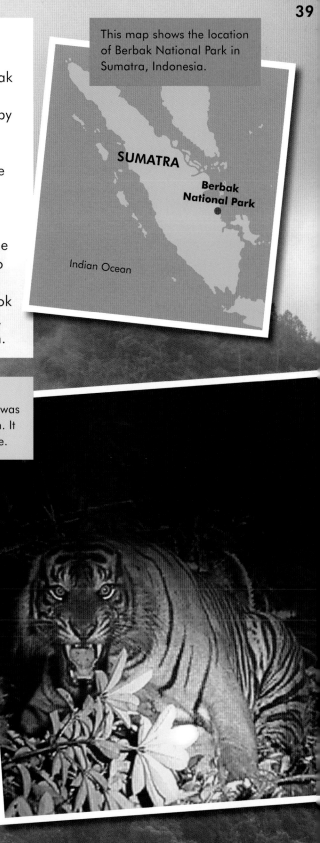

This map shows the location of Berbak National Park in Sumatra, Indonesia.

SUMATRA

Berbak National Park

Indian Ocean

This fierce Sumatran tiger was causing trouble at a village and was captured by a conservation team. It was safely moved to a new home.

TIGER TRANSPORT

Sometimes, a tiger starts raiding farms or villages, and scaring local people. But conservation organisations can help the Indonesian government to catch these tigers and move them away from where people live. They track the tiger, shoot it with a tranquiliser dart to make it sleep, and transport it by road or canoe. Before releasing the tiger, they fit it with a radio collar so that they can track where it goes and what happens to it.

CAN WE SAVE THE TIGER?

Will tigers still roam across Asia in ten, 20 or 50 years' time? Or will the remaining tigers, like their Caspian, Bali and Javan cousins, soon be extinct?

No more poaching

Some experts say that if things carry on as they are, tigers cannot survive in the wild for much longer. The poaching problem is so bad, it could wipe them out in as little as ten years. If that happens, tiger poaching will have to stop, once and for all. There will be no tigers to hunt. To save the tiger, conservationists have to try to get poaching to stop before then. Either way, the days of tiger fur trimmings and tiger bone medicines will soon be over.

Saving subspecies

It may be too late to save some subspecies of tiger, such as the South China tiger. Instead, some wildlife experts think we should focus all our efforts on the subspecies that have the best chance. The Amur tiger, for example, is breeding well in captivity, and surviving better in the wild than some other subspecies. It may be that some subspecies will become extinct, but a couple will be saved.

Will we one day remember tigers only from statues and photos?

Good news?

The Amur tiger has already stood right on the brink of extinction, in the 1940s. But conservation projects helped its wild population to grow again. Although the Amur tiger is still seriously endangered, this does show that wild tigers can recover their numbers – if they have enough space, and are protected from poachers.

So, while they still can, the thousands of conservation workers, scientists, park rangers, zookeepers, vets and experts who work with tigers will keep trying to save them.

Amur tigers may be able to increase their numbers further in the future.

This painting of a tiger in the snow is just one of thousands of artworks inspired by this beautiful creature.

CAT LOVERS

One thing that will help tigers is that they are well-known, admired and loved around the world. Most people think tigers are amazing, and don't want them to die out. The more zoos, TV programmes, and books like this one let people know about the tigers' plight, the more people will want to protect them.

ABOUT ZSL

The Zoological Society of London (ZSL) is a charity that provides conservation support for animals both in the UK and worldwide. We also run ZSL London Zoo and ZSL Whipsnade Zoo.

Our work in the wild extends to Russia, Bangladesh and Indonesia, where our conservationists and scientists are working to protect tigers from extinction. These incredible cats are part of ZSL's EDGE of Existence programme, which is specially designed to focus on genetically distinct animals that are struggling for survival.

By buying this book, you have helped us raise money to continue our conservation work with tigers and other animals in need of protection. Thank you.

To find out more about ZSL and how you can become further involved with our work visit **zsl.org** and **zsl.org/edge**

ZSL and other conservation groups are trying to make sure we don't lose tigers for ever.

Websites

Adopt a Tiger
www.zsl.org/adopttiger

Tiger SOS
www.zsl.org/tigers

Sumatran Tiger at ZSL London Zoo
www.zsl.org/sumatrantiger

Amur Tiger at ZSL Whipsnade Zoo
www.zsl.org/amurtiger

Places to visit

ZSL London Zoo
Outer Circle, Regent's Park,
London, NW1 4RY, UK
www.zsl.org/london
0844 225 1826

ZSL Whipsnade Zoo
Dunstable, Bedfordshire,
LU6 2LF, UK
www.zsl.org/whipsnade
0844 225 1826

We need to help tigers to have cubs, as this is the only way their numbers can grow.

Tigers may be fierce, but they are incredibly vulnerable and at risk.

GLOSSARY

adapt Change over time to suit the surroundings.

aggressive Easily annoyed or violent.

apex predator A hunting animal that is not eaten by other species.

breed Mate and have babies.

bamboo A type of very tall, strong grass-like plant.

black market Secret or hidden trading that is against the law.

camera trap A camera set up to take a photo when an animal comes near it.

captive breeding Breeding animals in zoos.

captivity Being kept in a zoo, wildlife park or garden.

cells The tiny units that living things are made up of.

conservation Protecting nature and wildlife.

continent One of the Earth's giant pieces of land.

critically endangered Very seriously endangered and at risk of extinction.

den A sheltered home or hiding place.

ecosystem A habitat and the living things that are found in it.

ecotourism Visiting wild places as a tourist to see wildlife.

enclosure A secure pen, cage or other home for a zoo animal.

endangered At risk of dying out and becoming extinct.

enrichment Something to make an area more fun and exciting.

extinct No longer existing.

gestation Length of time a baby grows inside its mother.

government The group of people in charge of a country.

GPS Short for Global Positioning System, a way of finding where you are.

habitat The natural surroundings that a species lives in.

habitat loss Damaging or destroying habitat.

habitat fragmentation Breaking up natural habitat into small areas.

HQ Short for headquarters, meaning a head office or control centre.

IUCN Short for the International Union for Conservation of Nature

logging Cutting down trees.

litter A group of baby animals all born to one mother at the same time.

mammal A kind of animal that feeds its babies on milk from its body.

mangrove A type of tree that can grow with its roots in water.

monitor To check, measure or keep track of something.

national park A protected area of land where wildlife can live safely.

oil palm A palm tree grown for oil that comes from its fruits.

paddock A meadow or open outdoor area.

park ranger Someone who patrols and guards a national park.

poaching Hunting animals that are protected by law and shouldn't be hunted.

population Number of people, or animals, in a particular place.

predator An animal that hunts and eats other animals.

prey Animals that are hunted and eaten by other animals.

solitary Preferring to live alone.

species A particular type of living thing.

status symbol An object that shows you have money and power.

studbook A record of the animals of a particular species born in captivity.

subspecies Different types of an animal within one main species.

sultan An Arabic or Asian ruler or king.

sustainable Able to be continued.

tapetum lucidum Latin for "bright carpet" – a silvery layer at the back of some animals' eyes.

territory An area that an animal considers its own.

tracking Finding or following wild animals by their signs and marks.

traditional Old-fashioned and dating back a long way.

tranquilising drug A drug used in a dart to shoot an animal to make it fall asleep.

ultrasound scan A way of using sound waves to look inside the body.

vitamins Chemicals that your body needs, found in some foods.

volunteer Someone who offers to do a job without being paid.

wildlife reserve A protected area of land where wildlife can live safely.

wildlife corridor A strip of natural habitat connecting wild areas.

ZSL Short for Zoological Society of London.

FIND OUT MORE

Books

Tigers in Danger by Michael Portman, Gareth Stevens Publishing, 2011

National Geographic Kids: Everything Big Cats by Elizabeth Carney, National Geographic, 2011

Tigers by Michael W. Richards and Hashim Tyabji, New Holland, 2008

Amazing Animals: Tigers by Sally Morgan, Franklin Watts, 2011

What's it Like to be a... Zoo Keeper? by Elizabeth Dowen and Lisa Thompson, 2010

ZSL Big Cats by Michael Cox, Bloomsbury, 2012

Websites

21st Century Tiger
www.21stcenturytiger.org

Great Cats at the Smithsonian National Zoo
nationalzoo.si.edu/Animals/GreatCats/default.cfm?cam=T1

Isle of Wight Zoo Tiger Webcam
www.isleofwightzoo.com/webcam.aspx

Places to visit

Dudley Zoo
2 The Broadway, Dudley, West Midlands, DY1 4QB, UK
www.dudleyzoo.org

Edinburgh Zoo
Corstorphine, Edinburgh, EH12 6TS, UK
www.edinburghzoo.org.uk/
0131 334 9171

Berlin Zoo
Hardenbergplatz 8, 10787 Berlin, Germany
www.zoo-berlin.de

San Francisco Zoo
Sloat Blvd. & Great Highway, San Francisco, CA 94132, USA
www.sfzoo.org

Isle of Wight Zoo
Yaverland Road, Sandown, Isle of Wight, PO36 8QB, UK
www.isleofwightzoo.com

Smithsonian National Zoo
3001 Connecticut Avenue NW, Washington, DC 20008, USA
www.nationalzoo.si.edu

INDEX

OTHER TITLES IN THE ANIMALS ON THE EDGE SERIES

www.storiesfromthezoo.com

Penguin
ISBN: HB 978-1-4081-4822-8
PB 978-1-4081-4960-7

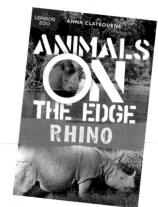

Rhino
ISBN: HB 978-1-4081-4823-5
PB 978-1-4081-4956-0

Gorilla
ISBN: HB 978-1-4081-4825-9
PB 978-1-4081-4959-1

Hippo
ISBN: HB 978-1-4081-4826-6
PB 978-1-4081-4961-4

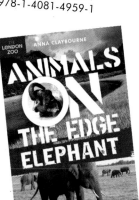

Elephant
ISBN: HB 978-1-4081-4827-3
PB 978-1-4081-4958-4